ACT NORMAL

AND DON'T TELL ANYONE ABOUT THE

RHINOCEROS
MAGNET

Christian Darkin

1

CHAPTER 1

I wish the man from the army had left my drawing of the rhino magnet. Now I can't remember exactly how it got made. I know it made a bit of a mess, but I think it's all OK now. I don't know why everybody got so upset.

I am writing this down anyway in case I need to make another one. Then I'll be able to work it out.

I don't think I will need to make another one, but you never know....

People in this story:

Me: I am Jenny. Two of my hobbies are experiments and saving the world. I make my best plans when things get really bad, which is lucky because in my house, things get really bad quite often.

When things get just a bit bad, I usually try to act normal. Acting normal means smiling and pretending there are no rhinos in the house, and all the walls are real.

Adam: Adam is my little brother. He doesn't like planning. He likes doing things instead. And he likes to make small things bigger – what he likes best is making a small mess and then making it really, really big.

Dad: Dad likes to clear up mess. At least, I hope he does because he has to do it a lot. He usually doesn't notice when things are just a bit bad, so acting normal works OK most of the time.

CHAPTER 2

It all started when my brother, Adam dropped his toy car into the pond. It was his best toy car and he cried.

I didn't want to put my hand into the pond to get it out because the fish are a bit dinosaury. This is because of something we did a few weeks ago, but that's not in this story.

I had a clever plan about how to get the toy car out. I got a piece of string. I got a big magnet. I put the magnet on the end of the string and I let it go down into the pond.

It took a few times of trying and then the magnet pulled the car out. I gave it back to Adam. Adam laughed. It was like fishing, but for cars.

When he played with his car, it stuck to his other cars. The car had got a bit like a magnet. I took the car back so that I could try a plan with it.

Adam cried again, but only for a bit, then he went and got his zoo animals.

Do you want to know my plan?

I got the magnet and rubbed it on all Adam's cars. Then they all stuck together. I had made all the cars into magnets. This was good.

I thought if I could make little cars into little magnets, then I could make Dad's car into a great big magnet. If I could make Dad's car into a great big magnet then I could make ALL the cars into great big magnets.

Then they would all stick together so only the one at the front would need to drive and the rest would follow it like a train

Then we wouldn't have to have so much pollution and we could save the world from global warming.

A lot of my plans are about saving the world because global warming is a BIG problem and I'm always trying to stop it.

Trying on toy cars was a good plan because real cars are hard to move about.

I found out that if I put the magnet cars all together they were stronger magnets. I found out that if I turned the cars round to point at each other, they pushed each other away.

This was good because it would stop them crashing when I made the big cars into magnets.

My brother likes to copy me. He started rubbing his toy animals together to try to make them magnets. But his toy animals are plastic and one was a lion and one was a rhino.

I told him that he was silly. I told him he couldn't make magnets because his animals were not the same like cars.

"OK," he said, "I'll try with two rhinos."

I thought it was OK because he only had one plastic rhino. Then he got his cuddly toy rhino and his plastic rhino and rubbed them together.

They did get a bit sticky, but that was because his cuddly rhino had some sweets in its fur, and some glue, and a bit of snot.

I thought it was all OK. But it wasn't
because do you know what happened the
next morning?

CHAPTER 3

The next morning Dad called us for breakfast. I was already dressed because I had been drawing my plans for a way to make all the cars in the world into magnets.

My plan is to put magnets in the roads so when the cars drive over them they rub over them and turn into magnets.

But I never did my plan because:

1) I need lots of magnets.
And
2) Adam's room was full of rhinos.

Adam was late for breakfast so Dad told me to get him.

I tried shouting, but he didn't come.

I tried shouting in an angry Dad way, but he still didn't come.

I tried saying if he didn't come he wouldn't get breakfast but he still didn't come.

I went up to his room and I pushed the door. It didn't open. I pushed it hard. It didn't open. Then I ran at it and it opened really quickly and I fell onto the floor.

Adam's room was full of rhinos. Not real rhinos - that would be silly. Adam's room was full of cuddly rhinos and plastic rhinos and toy rhinos of all kinds. There were even some balloon rhinos.

I don't know how, but Adam had made a rhino magnet with his toy rhinos and all the toy rhinos from all the houses in the town had come in the night and stuck to his rhinos.

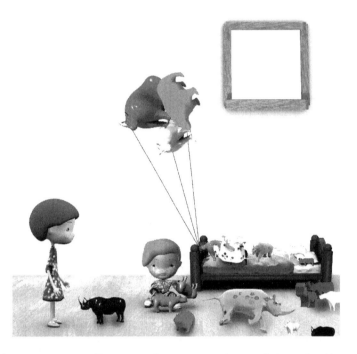

They were all together in a big rhino ball on Adam's bed. The rhino ball was so big it stopped me opening the door!

Adam was happy. He was playing rhino wars by putting rhinos in his Lego spaceships and rhino cranes by using rhinos to pick up other rhinos, and rhino dressing up by getting some big cuddly rhinos and putting his pants on them.

I told him he had to get ready for school.

I also told him he could not keep the rhinos.

"They are not your rhinos. You must give them back," I said (I have never said that before to anyone).

Adam looked sad, but he said, "OK," and we took lots of the rhinos to school, to give back to kids who had lost rhinos that night.

It was hard because we had to stuff them into our school bags and when we put the bags on our backs, they made us stick together.

Also, it was hard because at school we are only supposed to take one toy and we had lots, which we had to hide until we could find kids to give them back to.

If I had known what would happen next, I wouldn't have bothered...

CHAPTER 4

My brother, Adam likes bad things to happen. He is not bad, but he likes bad things when they are funny bad things.

When Adam sees something he can make bigger or louder or messier, he ALWAYS does.

When we got home from school, we still had some rhinos left, and they had got stickier by rubbing against each other in our bags.

Adam went up to his room. I had my plans to do for my magnet road so I didn't see him until story time.

On my way to bed, I saw into Adam's room. He had put all the sticky rhinos into a kind of magnet shape. He must have been rubbing ALL the rhinos together a LOT because now they were ALL stuck really strongly and like a really big rhino magnet.

Adam was sitting in the middle. He was smiling in his bad way.

"Dad!" I said. I was going to say, "Dad, Adam is building a big rhino magnet," but it sounded silly in my head and anyway, Dad said:

"Can we talk about it in the morning? It's very late," so I went to bed.

I knew there would be more rhinos in the morning, but I thought we could get rid of them, then I could have a big chat with Adam and it would all be OK.

I was wrong.

In the morning, Adam's room was full of rhinos. There were wooden rhinos and rubber rhinos and biscuits in the shape of rhinos and rhino posters.

There was even a robot rhino that Sam from school had got because his Granny was rich and he called it Rhino-zoid. It could walk and everything.

But that wasn't the problem.

The problem was that there was also a real rhino!

It was in Adam's room in the corner. It did not look happy, or sad. It just looked very, very big. It was bigger than his bed, and

it did not know why it was there. It just
made its ears flick and looked at me.

The rhino also smelled. It smelled of rhino,
which is a bit like the smell of zoo.

Adam was happy.

"I've got a rhino," said Adam at breakfast.

"Yes," said Dad. He thought Adam was talking about his cuddly rhino.

I didn't tell Dad he was talking about a real rhino. I knew we'd have to talk about that for a long time so I just acted normal.

I decided the best thing to do would be to hide the real rhino for now, and think of a plan.

Adam and I have got very good at hiding things. Strange things happen to us quite often (like the dinosaurs in the garden and the ice-cap in the library – which you can read about in other books).

We tried covering the rhino with the bed sheet but bits of rhino stuck out of the ends.

We tried dressing the rhino in one of my school uniforms so he could sit at the back in class, but he didn't look much like a girl. Anyway, we didn't have a wig and he really needed a wig.

In the end we used the wall trick. The wall trick is making a new wall in Adam's bedroom out of cardboard from the art box. We made the wall in front of the rhino and then we put the bed and the desk up against the new wall so it looked like the old wall.

Then we put all the other sticky rhinos in behind the wall.

Now Adam's bedroom looked the same as before, but just a bit smaller because one of the walls wasn't real and there was a rhino behind it.

We thought this would trick Dad for a day because he had to go to work and because we have done it before.

It worked! But the next morning things had got worse.

CHAPTER 5

I woke up early. I knew I would have to feed the rhino before school. I had looked on the Internet and found that rhinos eat grass. That was good. Our garden has lots of grass because Dad never cuts it because he never gets around to it.

When I looked out of the window, I thought that the rhino had got out. I knew it would be easy for the rhino to get out because the wall was only made of cardboard from the art box, but I hoped he would stay where he was.

I saw that there was a rhino in the garden, but then I saw that it was not the rhino from Adam's room. It was another rhino.

I knew that because it was next to two more rhinos, and there was another rhino standing in the flower bed. They were eating the flowers. I knew that there were not four rhinos in Adams room because we would have seen them.

This was strange because I thought rhinos only ate grass. The rhino in the flower bed did a big poo in the flowers.

Dad would probably be happy about the poo in the flowers because poo makes flowers grow, but he would probably not be happy that there were so many rhinos. He would also probably not be happy that they were eating the flowers.

Dad was in the kitchen making breakfast, but I needed a plan.

I got my brother out of bed. Rhino number 1 was still behind the pretend wall. Adam looked happy.

"I put all the sticky rhinos together," he said, "and I pointed them at the zoo."

I could see what had happened. Adam had made rhino number 1 and all the little rhinos into a big rhino magnet. Now, all the rhinos from the zoo were in the garden.

I wish I had never shown my brother about magnets.

I said, "We are going to have a long talk about this." I said it in my best serious voice.

He said, "I like rhinos."

I said, "I am going to hide all the rhinos. You have to act normal and keep Dad busy."

Adam is good at keeping people busy. He asked Dad for toast for breakfast.

When Dad got the toast, he asked for water.

When Dad got the water, he asked for pancakes.

When Dad got the pancakes, he said he had lost his sock.

When Dad got his sock, he was wearing his pants on his head.

Adam kept Dad busy until it was time to go to school.

At the same time, I went into the garden to hide the rhinos. Hiding rhinos is harder than you'd think. They are very much bigger than me and they do not move even when you push them very hard.

If you ever have to move a rhino, the best way is with a helicopter (you'll see that later in this book) but the second best way is by holding a bunch of grass out for it and letting it follow you.

We have a shed and there is a rhino space behind the shed. I put rhino number 2 there.

We have a bike cover and I put rhino number 3 under there.

We have some big flower pots and I put rhino number 4 behind them.

We have a space down the side of the house so I put rhino number 5 and rhino number 6 there.

Then I took rhino number 4 out because the flower pots didn't really hide her and I piled the compost from the compost heap over her. She looked like a big compost heap, but if you looked too hard, you could see she was very rhino shaped.

I hoped Dad would not notice. Then we went to school.

That was when things started getting tricky...

CHAPTER 6

On the way to school I saw lots of things had been knocked over. There were also a lot of rhino footprints in the road. They went all through town.

Dad saw them and looked at me and Adam, but we just acted normal and he didn't say anything.

At school, Alfred said he had heard on Newsround that the rhinos were missing from the zoo. "Is this you again?" he said.

People think strange things are always me. It's just because they normally are. This time it wasn't me though. It was Adam.

At break, I made a plan:

1) Clean up the town so rhino footprints didn't lead to our house.
2) Get all the sticky rhinos and move them a long way away from each other so they stop being a big magnet.
3) Get the real rhinos back to the zoo.
4) Have a long talk with Adam about not doing this again.

It was a good plan, but there were some bits missing in it.

The first part was easy. At lunch, I got Adam and we crept out of school.

I had seen a big road cleaning machine on the way to school. It had big brushes and a water squirter and yellow lights.

The man using it had gone to have his lunch.

Adam and I borrowed the machine. It was too big for me to drive and I don't know how to drive. I started to look at the machine and think how to work it.

Adam doesn't do thinking about things. He grabbed the steering wheel and pressed some buttons until it started moving.

We had a small bit of a fight over who was going to use the steering wheel.

Adam won. Adam likes going fast, but the cleaning machine would not go very fast, and it got a lot of things stuck in it because Adam drove through things not around them.

Things like dustbins and bikes and gardens.

By the time I got him to stop, we had made a bit of a mess. I got him to stop by pulling him out of the machine and letting a wall stop it. It was a good idea, but a bit messy.

The good thing was that the mess we had made covered up the mess the rhinos had made on their way to our house so the first part of the plan had worked. Sort of.

We left the mess and tried to act normal
going back to school. Nobody saw us, but
we saw somebody.

There was a man following the rhino
footprints. He had a big gun. When he got
to the mess we'd made with the cleaning
machine, he looked around. I hope he lost
the footprints in the mess.

I didn't like the look of him at all.

When I got home I put, "Man with gun following rhinos," into the Internet, and do you know what I found?

CHAPTER 7

The Internet told me that there are not very many rhinos left in the world.

There are two kinds of rhino in Africa. They are: the White Rhino – which is really light grey, and the Black Rhino which is really light grey as well.

There are not very many rhinos because there are lots of men with guns who keep shooting them. The men with guns are called poachers, and they shoot the rhinos to use their horns in medicine which doesn't work.

This is silly because rhino horns are really made from squashed hair. The lady who cuts my hair has lots of it all over her floor and she just throws it away.

The poachers could have that – and maybe then their medicine might work because little girl's hair hasn't been digging through mud. Except mine has sometimes.

Anyway, the Internet told me there are so many poachers and so few rhinos that soon there will be no rhinos at all.

There might even be no rhinos by the time you read this book. If there aren't, then look for a picture - rhinos have a horn on their nose and are very difficult to move.

So, I thought the man with the gun must have been a poacher.

That was really bad. Poachers follow rhinos by looking for their footprints, and then they shoot them.

CHAPTER 8

"What's that smell?" said Dad.

The right answer would have been, "That's the smell of a rhino, Dad," but I said, "What smell?"

Dad said, "It smells like a rhino." Then he said, "Jenny, is something going on?" He said it in the voice that meant, "Stop acting normal and really tell me," so I was about to tell him.

But, just then, Adam pointed out of the window. The poacher was in the street and he was not on his own. There were LOTS of poachers. They all had big guns and they were all coming along the street from different directions.

I ran to the back of the house, and saw that there were lots more poachers there! They were all coming towards the garden where rhinos 2,3,4,5 and 6 were hiding.

Dad said, "Jenny, is something going on?" again.

This time, I said, "I haven't got time to tell you. We've got to get all the rhinos into the house!"

That is something I've never said before, and I don't think anyone has ever said it to Dad before. But he is used to strange things happening, so he said, "OK, Jenny. How many rhinos are there?"

I said, "There are 6, but one of them is already inside."

Dad said, "OK," very quietly and he looked around.

"It's hidden," I said.

We all ran into the garden. Adam got rhino 2 from behind the shed. Dad got rhinos 5 and 6 from the side of the house, and I got rhino 3 from under the bike cover.

We all pushed our rhinos into the house through the back door.

Then we went back and got rhino 4. We brushed most of the compost heap off her, but she was still even smellier than a normal rhino, which is pretty smelly.

The poachers were looking over our garden wall by now and they saw us all get behind rhino 4 and push her into the dining room.

I could see them pointing their guns, but we got inside just in time.

We were safe for a little bit, but we were surrounded by poachers and we were in a house with 6 rhinos in it.

I needed a plan...

CHAPTER 9

I started by telling Dad everything. I told him about the car magnet (I still haven't done my magnet road plan). I told him about the toy rhinos, and about the rhinos from the zoo.

Then I told him about the pretend wall in Adam's room. Dad said he had thought Adam's room looked a bit smaller than normal, and a bit smellier.

I even told him about the cleaning machine and the poachers.

Dad said that bringing the rhinos into the house was probably the right thing to do. They were a bit messy, but the house was a bit messy anyway (That was because of when some toys came to life last week, but that is in another story).

Then we saw one of the poachers in the garden. He was shouting up to us.

"Send out the rhinos!" he shouted, "and we will leave you alone."

"What if we don't?" I shouted back.

"Then we will shoot you as well!" shouted the poacher.

I did not like either of those plans.

Neither did Dad. Neither did Adam.

So, I thought of a plan of my own.

I think of my best plans when things get
really bad. This plan was a bit dangerous,
but if it worked, it would be good.

It had to do with rhino bums. I drew a
picture of the plan and showed Adam and
Dad.

I told Adam to go and get all the sticky
rhino toys from his room. Dad and I got all
six of the rhinos to stand in a big circle.

They had to stand so that all their bums were in the middle of the circle and all their noses were facing out. We did it in the dining room because the dining room is open plan.

Then we put all the sticky rhinos together in a big bin bag and I gave it to Adam. Adam stood on top of rhinos 1 to 6 and started to run.

He ran round and round over the backs of all the rhinos dragging the big bag of sticky toy rhinos with him. He counted as he ran – 1,2,3,4,5,6,1,2,3,4,5,6 and he went faster and faster and faster.

We were making a very, very big rhino magnet, and the more Adam ran, the stronger the magnet got.

He ran and ran and sparks started coming out of the rhino magnet. The rhino magnet made this, "Wow, wow, wow!" noise getting louder and louder and louder.

And then there was another noise. A sort of thundering, rumbling noise that got louder and louder and louder.

We looked out of the window, and the poachers were all getting ready to shoot us. Then they heard the noise too. They stopped.

Then we all saw what the noise was. From all around, over the streets and the gardens and the fields, we saw rhinos. Lots and lots of rhinos running towards our garden from every side.

The rhino magnet was bringing thousands of them from all over the world!

There may not be very many rhinos left in the world but when you get them all in one place, and they are all running towards you they do look like a LOT.

The poachers all dropped their guns and ran, and the rhinos stomped all over the guns until they were just broken bits.

This was the dangerous bit of the plan. Now the rhinos were in the garden. There were thousands of rhinos stomping towards the house, and the house is not really big enough for even six rhinos.

If my plan didn't work, we would all be squashed.

I told Adam to stop running and we all turned rhinos 1-6 around so their heads were facing each other and all their bums were facing out.

Remember when I was making car magnets – when I turned them round, they pushed each other away?

Well, the same works for rhinos.

The moment we turned the rhinos so that their bums were facing out, all the thousands of rhinos in the garden and the thousands more in the road skidded around and started running away!

They ran back across the streets and gardens and fields. They ran faster and faster, back to the countries they came from.

In the end, there was just Adam, me, Dad and rhinos 1-6 left in the dining room.

CHAPTER 10

Dad said that the best way to get rhinos 1-6 back home to the zoo was by calling the army.

Adam loves it when Dad calls the army. He had a great time following them around pretending to be in the army.

The army came with big helicopters which were very loud and put the rhinos into rhino bags underneath the helicopters and flew away with them back to the zoo.

Then the leader of the army came and
asked me for the drawing I had made to
show Dad and Adam my rhino magnet plan.

He took the drawing away. "Why are you taking my drawing?" I said.

He said, "It's a secret." Then the army went, but they did not tidy up. Not one bit.

I can't tell you how messy the garden looked. It was the kind of mess you can only get by having thousands of rhinos in your garden.

Imagine the biggest mess you have ever seen, and then imagine a helicopter comes with another mess just as big and piles it on top. Then imagine the helicopter crashes on the mess.

It wasn't like that – it was worse than that.

I had planned to use my car magnets to save the world, but in the end, it didn't work. I only managed to save one kind of animal.

Next time, I will do better.

The end.

Things to do:

- If you liked this book, why not have a go at writing a review on Amazon?

- Please tell your friends on Facebook and in real life.

- There are lots of other "Act Normal" books. Why not just type "Act Normal" into Amazon and see what you can find?

- If you'd like the author, Christian Darkin to come and visit your school, you can get all the details at https://christiandarkin.wordpress.com/

The illustrations are by the author, but use some elements for which I'd like to credit and thank: www.obsidiandawn.com, kuschelirmel-stock, and waywardgal
Story and illustrations by © Christian Darkin

Act Normal and read more...

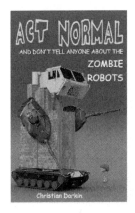

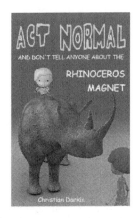

Made in the USA
Lexington, KY
21 November 2016